A Circus of Wonder

A. Carys

A. Carys

The characters and events portrayed in this book are fictitious. Any similarity to real persons, living or dead, is coincidental and not intended by the author.

No part of this book may be reproduced, or stored in a retrieval system, or transmitted in any form or by any means, electronic, mechanical, photocopying, recording, or otherwise, without express written permission of the publisher.

Copyright © 2024 A. Carys

All rights reserved.

BOOKS IN THIS SERIES

Of Doors and Betrayal

The Pickpocket and the Princess

The Master, My Wings, Our Service

'Cos This Is How Villains Are Made

A Circus of Wonder

A Sentence to Death

A Deal With The Devil

Let Her Go

The Three

Queen Rory, The Banished

A. Carys

A Circus of Wonder

DEDICATION

This one has slightly toasted chunks in it ;)

A. Carys

Beforehand

A. Carys

CHAPTER ONE

I grew up in the wonderful world of Circus performing.

My father was a Ringmaster. Rowyn Masters. The greatest Ringmaster of his time, the most powerful too. He was a force to be reckoned with, and that's what kept the fans coming back.

He started his circus, The Circus Wonder, as a way of cheering up my mother. He recruited performers from all over the world, the most talented ones he could find. Eventually, he started travelling with them, taking us, myself, my twin sister and my mother, with him to see the sights and the shows he put on. He made my mother laugh and clap and smile with pure happiness. He loved her so passionately, and he made sure that she knew that when he took on classes with the best Ringmaster he could find. Everything he did to grow The Circus Wonder was for her.

But he took on longer hours. He was always training. Always practising. His mentor showed him how to control the atmosphere around him. How to manipulate the audience's eyes into believing certain tricks and deceptions. I would watch from the rafters of the main tent. I'd copy the movements and try to learn everything as well, so that when the time came, I was prepared. I wanted to be just like my father when I was little. I admired him, and I admired his mentor, but just around the corner, everything was going to change.

My father quickly rose in popularity with his odd performances and his new performers with their almost ethereal like movements. People claimed they moved like ghosts, gliding across the stage and through their acts like they were walking on air.

Everything was perfect. Everything in mine and my sister's life was going well, until people decided they didn't like that our father was using magic to bring the circus to life. And I don't think any of us were prepared for the length that the protesters would go to try and eradicate the magic once and for all.

A. Carys

A Circus of Wonder

THEN, 1993 - 2020

A. Carys

CHAPTER TWO

January 1993

Today is my sixteenth birthday. A day I've been counting down to. Birthdays in The Circus Wonder are brilliant. You get a whole day, no matter what your role within the circus is, to yourself. I normally choose a day out in Amwin, but today I've chosen to spend it in the home tent. At least that's what I told my father.

His Mentor, the man responsible for training and moulding my father into the man he is, is on site today. So I'm spending my birthday watching today's Mentor session.

"Rin? Rin, wait for me," Rayna, my twin sister, whisper-yells as she runs to catch up with me.

"What?" I hiss, stopping and turning round to

face her.

"Where are you going?"

"Nowhere that concerns you."

She pouts. "You should be nice to me on my birthday."

"*Our* birthday," I say, correcting her. "And being nice to you isn't something a brother does. And I'm busy, so go away," I say and turn away from her, walking toward the back ladder of the main tent.

"Rin don't be like this. Please let me come with you," she begs, spinning me around and stopping me from walking away.

"No. We can't both watch, they'll know we're there."

"But I want to learn. You and I will one day run this place, and I'm not going to let you take on the magic all by yourself. You've seen what it's doing to dad. Let me in, share it with me."

I think about it, gnawing on my lip for a second. I want to share it with her, believe me I do. I want nothing more than to run this place with her, to have both of us follow in our father's footsteps. But at the same time, I'd rather take all of the magic. I'd rather take on the possession and ownership it takes on its host alone than let her go through it as well.

"Fine. You can come, but you need to stay quiet," I say and grab her wrist, dragging her behind me.

I pull her all the way to the ladder before climbing up before her. When I reach the top, I carefully and quietly unpeel a piece of the tent roof before slipping underneath it. I hold it open with one hand and aid Rayna with the other. Once she's fully on the wooden rafter, I close the roof panel.

We crawl along the rafters, being extra careful not to wobble or lose our balance. It's a nasty drop from this height, and while it might not kill us, it will definitely hurt. Luckily, we reach the metal gangway, quickly and without issue, before crawling onto it through the gaps in the side railing. From here, we have a completely unobstructed view of the ring below.

"Are they down there?" Rayna asks in a not so quiet voice, and I have to slap my hand over her mouth.

"Yes, but you need to learn to whisper. I will remove my hand if you agree to whisper properly," I say, practically muttering. She nods her head and I remove my hand.

We both carefully shuffle so that we are laying on our stomachs. Our heads peak out over the edge, and we have a direct view of our father and his Mentor. He's never formally introduced us to his Mentor, but every time I watch them, I marvel at the talent. My father is learning from the best man in the business. He's truly a master of magic, his hands moving quickly and smoothly as he controls the atmosphere around him.

We watch from above, taking in the sight of our father mastering the art of the Circus. His Mentor helps guide his hands in a very particular pattern as he starts to gather the magic that resides in the tent. It's enchanting and I struggle to look away.

"He's very talented," Rayna mutters, and I nod in agreement.

"I think he's hoping to make mum smile again."

She looks at me with tears in her eyes. "You really think so?"

I nod. "She's always loved magic and fantasy. Maybe this will bring them back together?"

"Rin? Rayna?" our father calls. We both peer over the edge and see him looking up at us.

We look at each other and then look down sheepishly. We give our father a little wave and he rolls his eyes playfully.

"Can you come down here, please?" he asks, and we nod. We carefully scramble to our feet and make our way back down the way we came. Back onto the wooden rafters before climbing down the ladder and heading round the tent. We step through the front entrance and walk until we are standing in front of our father.

"You two are trouble. *You.*" He points his finger at me. "Told me you would be in the home tent. And you, Rayna, told me you'd be with Alita and Edith," he says, scolding us. "Despite that, I'm glad you're here actually. I need you two to go back to the home tent and tell your mother to put on her prettiest dress. Then I want you to bring her here for tonight's show."

"We can do that," Rayna says.

"Good. And make sure you wear your nicest outfits as well, tonight we are celebrating a new beginning."

"Yes dad," we say in unison before he dismisses us. We sprint out of the tent and toward our house to get ready.

Rayna and I do exactly what our father said. We find our mother in the home tent, sitting on their bed with a sketchpad and pencil in her hands. We tell her exactly what father said before going and getting dressed ourselves.

I meet my mother and sister outside the main tent, and we all enter together. The crowds that line the metal bleachers are all murmuring and laughing as they patiently wait for the show to start. The three of us take up our normal seats, three cushion clad, reserved spaces in the front row.

"What has your father planned?" my mother asks.

"I'm not sure, but I think it has something to do with his Mentor."

She smiles meekly and sighs. She's always hated the way dad spends so much time with his Mentor. Sometimes it comes, not only, between them as a couple, but also us as a family unit. He's missed birthday dinners, the second anniversary of our little sister's death, and Christmas celebrations in favour of learning from his Mentor.

It's not long until our father steps into the ring. He takes up his place on the podium and the lights over the audience dim. A spotlight singles him out.

"Welcome, ladies and gentlemen. Tonight is the start of a new era at The Circus Wonder and I'm thrilled to have you all here to witness it."

The audience claps and hoots.

"For the last two years, I have been working with a Mentor who chose me to take on the gift of storytelling. The gift of enchanting audiences through the acts that they witness during their visits here. I have been gifted the ability to entertain more than any other circus currently active." He pauses for a second, hoping off of his podium. "But that's not entirely the main reason. My wife has waited two years for me to return to her, to devote my time to her and our family again. And I have waited two years to see her smile like she used to. We've faced challenges that took a lot from us, but we came out the other side. So tonight's performance is dedicated to her, to our new beginning, and to a new round of successful tours."

Everyone claps again as my father comes over and leans over the raised edge. He climbs over and takes a seat on the edge.

"This is for you, my love. I've done all of this for you because I want to see you smile again. To hear you laugh properly and with your heart. The loss of our baby girl was hard, so I also want to dedicate this to our baby, who would've been one of the greatest performers to ever live," he says to her, mentioning the loss of our little sister. It's something that set a wedge between them and was what, ultimately, brought about the tension in their marriage.

Don't get me wrong, I miss her too, and while I wouldn't tell anyone in my family, I visit her grave every two weeks to just talk to her. To share with her the magic I get to witness every day.

Father leans in and kisses my mother's cheek before rolling sideways off the edge of the ring. He lands perfectly on his feet, before waving his arms up and clapping his hands together. The lights turn off and I hear the audience around us breath in a breath of anticipation.

Faint dots from the spotlights, coloured with gels, start to fade in and out of focus. It takes a few seconds before the spotlights directly above begin to flicker with bright white light. The whole ring then lights up and my father's best performers stand in the middle. Alita, Edith, Harry, Tarron, Josie and Alfie. They stand in the middle, in a line and posing. They wait for the music to start which is played by our live band.

The music kicks in quickly just as the light flickers again, and I just catch sight of the performers taking up their secondary positions. When the lights stop flickering, Alita is standing on the podium in the centre of the ring, her silver outfit sparkling under the lights. Her entire being has been doused in silver products; silver gemstones have been stuck around her eyes in the shape of wings, her hair has been combed upwards messily and sprayed with silver, along with a dusting of silver lipstick and glittery eyeshadow.

Alita normally performs as a clairvoyant. She predicts the future for our chosen audience members and would perform tarot readings with mind blowing accuracy. But tonight, she's doing something different. She's holding up a grainy photograph of Edith, our human puppet act. She calls for Edith to come out of the wings as well. Edith does so, only briefly though as she twirls and bows before the audience. As Alita brings the attention back to herself, I see Edith slip back behind the curtains at the side. Alita takes a deep breath before appearing to channel the magic of the circus. She seamlessly transforms herself into Edith before quickly turning herself into my father.

The crowd *oohs* and *aahs* at her performance, clapping and shouting encouraging words. Alita seems to flourish under their praise as she ups the skill level of her transformations. She takes on the appearance of a bird, a great snowy owl with beautiful, speckled wings. She hovers just above the podium, flapping her wings with delicate grace before lowering herself back down. The audience claps, shouting and cheering as the lights flash off. When they turn back on, Alita is back to her human form. She bows and blows kisses before walking out of the ring.

As the applause dies down, Alfie wheels a

platform into the centre of the ring. Edith stands on top of it, bent in half at the waist with her arms and head hanging limply.

"Ladies and gentlemen, children of all ages. Observe the music box before you. Observe and watch as my fire brings her to life," Alfie says as he pulls his matches from his pocket.

He makes a show of pointing to the balls of kinder pinned onto his shirt. He strikes a match and lights one of the balls, letting it crackle and spit before he pulls the pin and lets it roll down his arm. The ball bounces off his arm and lands perfectly on target. The little flames ignite the torch head and the small fire rages. Edith twitches. Alfie repeats the same routine with three other torches. Once the final one is lit, Edith bursts to life very briefly before powering back down.

Alfie gasps dramatically which makes the audience laugh. "Sorry. My bad, let me try again."

This time, he lights another four torches before turning a key at the back of the music box. Edith powers back up, and the platform she's standing on starts spinning. She dances and entertains which makes the audience clap.

"Now, this act is normally a little plain, but tonight, thanks to our Ringmaster, we've made it a little more entertaining. Behold the doll whose encased in her cracks, she's old and worn out, but with a little helping hand she'll flourish."

Alfie lights up the once invisible cage around Edith. He blows at the fire, and it appears to engulf Edith. The fire dances around her, engulfing her in flames that should burn her, but they don't. As the fire extinguishes itself, it reveals her without any of the cracked makeup. Her dress is complete, no longer with hanging tatters. She's whole again and the audience claps loudly.

"Behold the doll who's whole again and watch as she dances around the steps of fire," he says as he blows a match, and it lights up a series of clear steps. He offers his hand to Edith, and she takes it as she steps up onto the first step. She marvels at it before letting go of Alfie's hand and practically skips up the others.

How aren't her feet burning, I wonder.

When she reaches the top, she wobbles and falls

headfirst off toward the floor. But she doesn't hit the floor as Harry, our Jester, seems to appear out of thin air. He catches her. He spins her around like she weighs nothing before throwing her back into the air. Tarron swoops past just in time from his trapeze and catches her.

While the audience claps and pays even more attention than before, I sneak a glance at my mother. She's smiling and her eyes are eagerly tracking the movements in the ring. She claps along with the audience, and I can see her eyes light up every time something exciting happens. She looks happy, excited even, and it makes me wonder whether this is enough to begin to heal the rift between her and my father.

The show continues and it only gets more exciting. Once Edith is returned to her box, and her clothes transform back to the tatty dress she started in, Alfie rolls her out of the ring and doesn't come back.

Josie and Tarron, our aerial artists, walk onto the stage to close the show. They swing and leap and throw each other across the performance space before they land on the floor of the ring. They're entangled with each other, holding onto each other, before some kind of swirling magic makes them disappear. The spotlights turn off as well, leaving the tent in total darkness.

The audience gets up from their seats, clapping and hooting as my father appears on the podium. He bows and beckons for his performers as well. They all bow as well, taking in the cheers for their performance.

My father thanks the audience for coming and says that he hopes they will return to witness even more magic. He tells of the travelling he intends to do over the next six months before returning to this very site ready to showcase the final, most spectacular show of the new season. A way of closing out his new legacy with a bang.

But what he didn't see coming was the letters, the petitions and the threats of investigation from the public. It turns out, a few of the first audience members who witnessed his new show didn't like the idea of magic. *Real* magic. And what began as harmless paper threats, ended in graffiti and property damage.

CHAPTER THREE

31st July 1993

Six months of semi quiet protests have turned into chaos.

Tonight, we are back where we started, Amwin. After six months on the road, my father has planned a spectacular closing show. We always start and finish our tours in Amwin. After all, it is the home of The Circus Wonder. And it also happens to be the place where we receive the most protesters.

Father has Rayna and I setting up barriers around the entire outer edge of the site. The barriers are for ours and the guests safety after a spate of damages started appearing around the circus. Not all of the protesters are aggressively shouting, those are the ones we don't mind hanging around during business hours. It's the protesters which try to grab visitors and forcefully shove their Anti-Circus Wonder flies into their hands. It's only midday and the protesters are out in full force. A smaller crowd has greeted us at each tour location we've been to in the last few months. They all bring posters and A3 paper signs which they wave around while chanting. This crowd is no different.

Ban magic, there's no place for it in this world. Their favourite chant, as though magic is something that can just be gotten rid of. It's everywhere, and how do they know they or someone in their family hasn't come into contact with magic.

Burn the witch. Another favourite of theirs. They seem to believe that my mother is the one who is supplying the magic. And that by looking back in history they've found something to indicate that my mother is a descendent of witches.

Arrest Mr Masters for crimes against the natural world. Well that's a new one.

"Don't you have lives to be tending to?" Rayna shouts at the crowd as she connects the final barrier.

"We do, but our protests against The Circus Wonder are far more important," says one protester.

"How can we live normal lives when we're in danger of having magic used against us?" shouts a second protestor.

"Cool, well, no one is using magic in your daily lives, so go find something better to waste your time on," Rayna yells back.

"Hey, could you move some of the leaves out of the way while you're standing there, they keep getting all over the tent floors," I shout at them as we walk away.

Rayna and I chuckle to ourselves as the crowd starts shouting obscenities at us. And we don't let that stand, we both turn at the same time and stick our fingers up at them. The crowds have repeatedly tried to intimidate us through their words. They try to poison our minds against our father, but they're never successful, and they never will be. Our family unit is stronger and closer than ever, and nothing they say will ever change that.

"Ah, good. I was wondering if you two had finished the barrier yet?" Father asks as we enter the main tent.

"All done. And a little bit of crowd hazing at the

same time," I tell him, and he smiles while shaking his head.

"What have I told you about provoking them?"

"Not to. But it's fun. They're so serious and so invested in their silly protests that they are, ultimately, boring and unfulfilled people," says Rayna, a mischievous glint sparkling in her eye.

Father shakes his head. "They might be boring and unfulfilled, but I want you to stop provoking them. The last thing we need is one of them getting bold and taking a swing at either of you."

"Yes father," we say before he tells us to go and change ready for the performance.

Rayna and I stand in the wings, patiently waiting to step into the ring.

In the months that we were on tour, the two of us took on the challenge of learning sleight of hand. We've always wanted to be a part of the acts on stage, so once father deemed our act as *perfection*, we were added to the beginning of the show to warm up the crowd. Tonight will be our fourth performance, and we hope it will be our best.

"Tonight, ladies and gentlemen, we've two special guest stars. My children, Rayna and Rin, will be performing for you tonight."

The audience claps which is our cue. We step from the wings and meet each other in the middle. We shake hands and turn to the crowd.

"As a warmup to the evening, we'll be performing some of our favourite tricks," I tell the audience as I pull a pack of cards from my pocket. "This pack of cards is new, brand new to the point they haven't been unwrapped," I say as I peel back the cellophane wrap, scrunching it up and shoving it in my pocket. I then open the pack and empty all of the cards into my hand.

"For our first trick this evening, I will make my sister disappear. This is a favourite one of mine, a little peace and quiet," I joke as I fan out the cards and wave them in front of the audience.

I then stand one shoe length in front of Rayna, waving the cards around her front and over the top of her head to show there's nothing there.

"And now, goodbye Rayna," I say as I let go of the cards the way we practised. Waving them in the air and then letting them go as though they were water coming out of a fountain. The audience *oohs* as the last card hits the floor and Rayna is gone. The crowd claps and a few of them peer around the tent to see where she'll reappear.

"Now, while I collect my cards, I want you all to think of a card. Don't tell me, don't whisper it to your friends or family," I tell them as I pick up the cards. "Just keep it to yourself."

Once all the cards are back in my hand, I fan them out and mix them up a few times before heading close to the audience. I approach a couple and fan out the cards, the figures and symbols facing down at the floor.

"Ma'am, if you'd be so willing as to choose a card?" I ask and she nods. I hold out the fan and she takes one from the end. "Now I've no idea what card is where, so here is the interesting part," I step back till I'm in the middle of the ring and standing next to the prop table.

"Some of you may have noticed this table. It contains four more unopened packs of cards." I place down the fan of cards and open two of the packs. I mesh them together and show the audience my next trick.

"Now, as much as I don't want to, I guess I'll bring Rayna back. She has a few tricks of her own she wants to show you. And as much as I like the peace and quiet, I can't rob her of her moment in the spotlight. Everyone count with me back from three,"

THREE

TWO

ONE

I throw the cards into the air and let them fall in a flurry of red and black and white. It makes a bigger mess than the first drop but by the time the cards hit the floor Rayna is back, and this time she's holding up a card high above her head.

"In my hand I hold the same card as the audience member my brother chose. In my hand, I hold the Eight of Hearts," she says, turning the card round to show the audience. They all clap, and I quickly make my way over to where the lady with the card is sitting.

"My lovely audience assistant, what card are you holding?" I ask her.

"The Eight of Hearts," she says, slightly shocked

as she shows both me and the audience her card. Everyone claps and whoops and we bow.

I take a step back, taking a seat on the side of the ring to let Rayna perform her tricks. She performs quite a few sleight of hand tricks on the audience. Pulling a stack of cards out of thin air before predicting what card an audience member was thinking of. She makes the deck of cards levitate, one card at a time until they look like a ladder. She finishes by throwing a flashbang down on the ground next to her. Both she and the cards disappear, signalling the end of our act.

We meet in the middle of the ring before bowing to the audience. They applaud loudly as we thank them and tell them to enjoy the rest of the show. We exit the ring together, heading up to the back row of the audience where the performers can sit and watch the rest of the show.

We watch the rest of the show. All the lights, the jumping, the dancing and the dangerous tricks the main cast have been practising while on tour all come together to close out our season. It's the best show we've ever done; and the standing ovation the audience gives at the end of the show backs up that thought.

For some reason, a ball of emotion bubbles inside of me. The Circus Wonder has gone back to how it was, the family feel, the enjoyment of the audience and the closeness of my parents as they step out onto the stage and bow. They've reunited and become so much more in sync with one another. Rayna and I don't just have a mother and father as part of our family, we have the entire circus as our family, and I couldn't feel any more grateful.

"A toast to our final performance of the season."

Everyone lifts up their glass, clinking them and cheering. We're all sitting around a large table mother and father set up after we closed down the circus for the night. Father ordered a royal feast's worth of takeaway, and it arrived a few minutes ago. He spread the food containers out on the table. Everyone came along and took a seat around the table, and once everyone was settled, my father stood and made a toast.

"So what now? What happens during the break?"

Alita asks.

"We'll work on the acts. We'll improve them and we will work on levelling up all of our skills. You'll all have a three month block of holiday to rest and recuperate. Then we'll start with one month on and one month off until the start of the new season," says my father. Everyone nods.

"Rowyn are you going to announce it?" my mother asks him.

"Are you sure? We don't have to if you don't want to."

"I want to. It's the right time."

He nods and stands up again. Rayna and I exchange confused looks as he begins speaking.

"You were all with us when we lost our daughter a few years ago. It broke something within, not only our family unit, but our circus family. But over the last six months, we've all come back together. We've worked on ourselves, and we've all come back together stronger. So, we are happy to announce that we're having a baby." Everyone claps and congratulates our parents. "Now we know we're not as spritely as we used to be when Rayna and Rin were born, but we're both looking forward to the new addition to our family," father says and he sits back down next to our mother, pressing a gentle kiss to her cheek.

I'm lost for words.

"Did you know anything about this?" Rayna whispers to me.

"No, no idea. I wouldn't have been able to guess this was something that was going to happen."

Our father beckons Rayna and I to join him and our mother in the corner of the room.

"We wanted to tell you at the same time as we told the rest of the company. We hope you don't mind that we did that," he says as he wraps an arm around our mother's waist.

I smile at both of them. "It's fine."

"Are you sure?" mother asks nervously.

I nod and glance at Rayna.

"We're happy for you both, and I think I speak for both of us when I say we are both very excited to have another sibling," Rayna says before she goes in for a hug. Mother embraces her and then gestures for me to join in.

"No, you know I'm not really a hugger," I say jokingly.

"Get in here," my father orders while shaking his head playfully.

I roll my eyes and step forward into the hug. We take that moment as a family to be present, to reiterate our love for each other before returning to the table.

The rest of dinner is filled with laughter, and most of the people round the table getting slightly tipsy. Eventually, we all abandon the table and have an odd dance party in the middle of the ring. Everyone is celebrating and enjoying what has been a ridiculous amount of success.

Throughout the makeshift party, people start to taper off. First a few of the stage crew, who help make the show possible disappear. Then the main cast start to head back to their shared space after telling my father they are going to call it a night.

Finally, it's just me, Rayna, mother and father. We chat about the baby, about the future that is calling to us and the circus. Eventually, when mother says she's going to retire for the night, father decides to go with her. Which just leaves me and Rayna. We don't stay out much longer, just long enough to try as many of the different alcohols, that have been left lying around, as we can. Once we've tested each one, we giddily stumble back to our room.

"Are you happy about another sibling?" she asks as she changes in the bathroom.

"I guess. It'll be nice to do all the things we didn't get to do with Riya."

"Yeah," she says and comes out of the bathroom. "Do you think that is the reason they worked so hard on their issues? They were so close to divorce that maybe this surprise baby pushed them to become better."

"Remember that everything started to look up after the first performance where he pledged full dedication to mother. I think all the progress they've made up till this point was what led to the baby. They'd have actually had to have liked each other a lot to be able to make the baby in the first place."

She grimaces. "Ew, please don't talk to me about our parents sex life. Oh god, images," she says with a grimace before pretending to vomit. I laugh.

"Anyway, night," I say as I crawl under the duvet

of my bed.

"Night." She switches off her bedside lamp and the room becomes enveloped in darkness.

Rayna is asleep within minutes, light snores coming from her side of the room. But sleep doesn't come to me. I twist and turn in bed, but for some reason, I can't seem to relax as something heavy settles in the pit of my stomach.

I watch the clock, midnight becomes one - oh - clock, which becomes two - oh - clock, which finally becomes three - oh - clock. I can't get to sleep, no matter how much I twist and turn to try and get comfortable. I huff and fling the duvet off of my body. I carefully get out of bed, sneak out and down the stairs of the home tent before walking out of the door. I quietly run across the clearing before jumping over one of the barriers. I scramble to the second tree line before scaling up the hidden ladder my father put there.

Many years ago he built a treehouse on this plot of land, he wanted something for Rayna and I to be able to play in when we weren't old enough to take up jobs in the circus. It's a little rickety now, the wooden floorboards are slightly musty, and the corners are covered in cobwebs, but it's still standing.

I wiggle through the hatch of the treehouse before collapsing on the wooden floor. I lay there for a second before crawling over to the window. I take a seat and look out at the window, instantly feeling calmer. But the calm doesn't last long when flashes of light start filtering through the trees and spilling into the clearing. I duck down, hiding. I can hear them faintly talking and when I peak back through the window I see three groups of them, each one heading into the home tents. I think they've all disappeared, but I catch sight of one heading toward the main tent.

I shimmy carefully across the treehouse and back down the ladder just as short screams sound from the home tents. As quickly as they all start screaming, they stops. And then the fire starts. I watch in horror as my home goes up in flames. I hide between the trees and watch as they all come out, dusting off their hands before disappearing back into the trees.

I'm panicking, and the first thing I do is run back into the room I share with my sister. She's on her bed, face up. I run to her side and check her over, I see no visible injuries until I pull back the duvet. The once white sheets are now covered in blood. Three stab wounds decorate her torso.

"Rayna? Wake up please," I beg, tears now streaming down my face as I try to both staunch the bleeding and shake her awake. But she doesn't move, not one inch, and her chest doesn't rise or fall. "Ray-Rayna," I whimper as I stop trying to revive her. She's gone.

I cry out as I collapse to my knees. *My sister is dead, my best friend.* The smoke from the fires burns at my throat and eyes. I start to choke; deep guttural coughs consume me as I stumble to my feet and head to my parents room. The situation is the same when I pull back the covers. Three stab wounds each, all on the torso, all with no pulse when I check.

My mother, father and baby sibling. My twin. All of them gone. Dead. What about the others?

I stumble again as I leave the room, affected by both the smoke and all of the emotions swirling inside of me. I scrape a few coins from the table by my parents' bedroom door. I shove them into my pyjama trouser pocket. Tears are still streaming down my face as I make my way out of the home tent. I stumble across the grounds and make my way out to the street. I trip over a loose pavement slab as I finally reach a pay phone.

I shakily take out a couple of coins from my pocket and place them into the coin slot. I then pick up the receiver and dial nine - nine - nine.

"Nine - nine - nine, what service do you require?"

I swallow, trying to form words. "Uh, uhm, all of them. I think. But they're dead so I don't– I don't know."

"Sir, please remain calm. Can you tell me where you are?"

"Amwin, Wesley Lane, in the forest clearing. The Circus Wonder, my father is the owner."

I can hear her clicking on her keyboard before she talks again.

"Now, what's your name and can you tell me what happened?"

"Rin Masters. And they came in, i– in and they stabbed everyone and then set it all on fire. They're dead, they killed my family, and my home is burning down."

"Okay, sir, I've got the police, ambulance and fire on the way to your location now. They're not far away."

I nod.

I need to get out of here.

I need to get away.

"Sir? Are you still there?"

"I have to go," I say as nausea rolls through me, strong and almost to the point where I keel over.

"No, no sir, please stay on the li–"

"No. No I need to go, I'm sorry." I put the receiver down and head back into the forest.

I trip over roots and walk into many branches on my way back to the clearing. Even from the second tree line I can see the flames as they consume the fabric tents. I manage to climb the ladder to the treehouse, and I feel all the emotions hit me again all at once. It's all consuming and everything hurts. Tears burn my eyes and I empty my stomach out the window.

I can see the lights and hear the sirens of the emergency services. I hear their boots on the twig and leaf covered ground. I can hear them dragging their fire hoses. I collapse on the floor as pain overtakes all of my senses. My whole body aches, my nerves feel like they're on fire. They fizzle and my whole body burns, and nausea builds up my throat again. It feels like I'm having some kind of seizure. The flashing lights from the emergency service vehicles sting my eyes. Pain explodes in the back of my head as my muscles contract and twitch as pins and needles take over. My body runs hot, and then cold, alternating to the point where I'm dry retching. Everything hurts and I want it to stop.

Make it stop, I beg. Please, just– just make it stop.

The hoses turn off after a while and then I hear them calling my name. But I don't respond, I don't want to be found. I want to stay here and cry and wallow in my feelings.

My family is dead. My whole family.

Once I come back to myself, the pain having subsided enough that I can move my fingers individually. My tears and sadness turn into hatred. Thoughts of great violence and revenge fill my mind. I'm going to make each and every one who came here tonight pay for what they did to my family.

CHAPTER FOUR

3rd August 1993

One day, six hours and thirty minutes is how long it takes me to regain control of my body.

Two days, six hours and thirty minutes since the Circus was set on fire and everyone was murdered.

I sit in one of the back booths of the local cafe. The television set is playing the news again, and they're talking about what happened.

"Two days ago emergency operators received a call from the son of respected Ringmaster Rowyn Masters. Emergency responders were sent to the woodland clearing next to Wesley Lane. Upon arriving at the clearing, they were shocked to find more that than eighty percent of the buildings were on fire."

As much as I don't want to listen, I need to know

if anyone survived. I was fully immobilised inside of the treehouse, so I didn't see how many bodies they dragged out of the wreck. *If they managed to pull any out*, the voice at the back of my mind says.

"The fire brigade contained the fire quickly, but it appears that everyone inside was already dead before the fires were started. Detective Inspector Benjamin Joy gave a statement to the press which stated that *every resident in the tents had been stabbed at least three times and would've died quickly from a combination of blood loss and smoke inhalation.* He also said that *everyone was accounted for bar the only son of Rowyn and Talia Masters, Rin Masters.* The last anyone heard from him was his urgent call to nine - nine – nine. Violet Bowler spoke to the operator who answered the call."

They play a recording of the call and speak to the woman I spoke to. Tears build in my eyes again as I listen to the recording of my voice. The panic, grief and sadness in my voice are so strong that it makes me cry again. That call is a bit of a blur to me, so hearing it out loud brings up all kinds of thoughts.

"As of this morning, Greater Amwin Hospital has

confirmed the deaths of nine people who were pulled from the burning tents."

Talia Masters,
Rowyn Masters,
Rayna Masters,
Alita Annacroft,
Alfie Reynolds,
Edith Severo,
Harry Akei,
Tarron Day,
Josie Brownly.

Their photographs appear on the screen as the newsreader says everyone's names. Tears make my vision completely blurred as I see their faces again.

"It isn't clear whether there will be a funeral, but Mr Masters spokesperson has said that the family lawyer is currently dealing with the distribution and preservation of the land. A helpline has been created for those affected by the sudden, and rather destructive death of valued members of the Amwin community. The helpline can also be contacted, and is encouraged to be used, by the only surviving member of the Masters family, Rin. Police search teams are still looking for the 16 year old…"

"Sir are you alright?" asks a waitress, and I look up at her, clearly having attracted her attention because of my sobbing and sniffing.

"Yeah, yeah I'm fine. I have to go," I say as I get up from the booth and leave the diner.

I head back down through the town and onto Wesley Lane before ducking into the forest. I head toward the treehouse, climbing the ladder and heading over to the window. In the lowlight of the late afternoon, I have a clear view of the space. Sadness bubbles away inside of me.

The entire place has been blocked off with police tape, and the stench of smoke still sits heavily in the air. Everything looks grey and dark, compared to the vibrant colours and lights that were all around the place beforehand. Everything is gone. I've not been inside yet; I keep meaning to. I want to collect some of my stuff, my family's stuff, so that I can live comfortably in the treehouse. Unfortunately, I keep noticing the odd police officer walking around the site, so for now, I'm staying put.

※

It takes two weeks for the authorities to leave the site alone.

In that time, I manage to sneak into the now charred kitchen of the home tent a handful of times. I took anything that didn't need to be cooked and things that weren't yet out of date. I also grabbed the surviving snack boxes that father used to keep backstage in the main tent. I ration the food and, thankfully, have unlimited access to the outside fountains which somehow managed to survive the fire.

I make my way down the ladder and over to my family's home tent. I head up the stairs and into what was my bedroom. The bloody sheet from Rayna's bed has been removed, all of the blood that had dripped onto the floor has been cleaned up as well. Surprisingly, there's only a little bit of fire damage in here. I move out of the room and head to my parents room. The same thing has happened here, the blood has been cleaned up and only the corners of the floorboards show the slightest bit of fire damage.

I move through all of the tents, checking out the condition of them. Out of all eight tents we have on the property, only three of them are completely unusable, which is surprising considering the amount of fire I saw spreading across the grounds.

As I head back toward my family's home tent, the sound of tires on gravel catches my attention. I duck behind a full panel of fabric and try to quiet my breathing.

"Rin?" a man calls out.

"Rin, I know you're living here. You don't need to be scared of me because I'm your family's lawyer. Your father put me in charge if something were to happen to him and the circus."

My father told me about him. *Mr Myles*. My father sat down with me a few months ago, almost like he knew something was going to happen to him and the circus. He gave me a word, a word that only myself, my father and Mr Myles would know. I assume he gave the same word to Rayna and my mother, a precaution just in case they were to survive.

"What word did my father give you?" I shout before moving to the other side of the tent. If this wasn't Mr Myles then I wasn't going to wait and let him find me.

"Obelisk. The word he gave me was obelisk."

I sigh, feeling relieved. I step out from my hiding place and approach him. He's a slightly older man, hair greying around the edges and his back slightly hunched over. His face is covered in lines and round glasses sit primly on the bridge of his nose.

"I'm Mr Myles, it's a pleasure to finally meet you," he says as he reaches out to shake my hand.

"Nice to meet you too." I shake his hand.

"I'm sorry it couldn't be under better circumstances, and my condolences for your losses."

"Thank you."

We talk some more before he asks if there is somewhere we can sit so that he can go through some things with me. I guide him to the main tent, where the performing ring is still partially standing. We sit on the edge, and he talks me through everything that is going to happen now that my father has passed.

He tells me that I'm now the owner of the plot of land the circus is on and that I am to try and restore as much of it as I can. Father wants me to restore the Circus and then run it, claiming that I already should have felt the power transfer, which would've happened the moment my father's heart stopped beating.

That must've been what the headache, the seizure and the pain was all about, I think to myself.

"All of this? I have to look after all of this?"

"Yes. If you choose not to, I have instructions to sell the land to the highest bidder."

"NO," I yell. "No, I'll look after it."

"Good to hear. Your father left me with a box of items that will help you live safely and comfortably. You've also inherited your fathers fortune. A fortune he told me he'd been saving since he started working in the circus. I have all the information here." He hands me an envelope before telling me to come with him to his car to grab the box.

When we reach his car, I see a variety of urns sitting carefully secured in the boot.

"Ah, you've seen the urns. I was going to go over them last. Your father told me that if anything were to happen to him and the people in the circus, their bodies were to be cremated and the urns returned to the Circus land in the hopes that their souls can rest peacefully here."

I nod.

"Is that everyone?"

He nods. "Yes. Where would you like to put them?"

"I'm not– I'm not sure actually. Could you leave them here and I'll find a place for them?"

He nods. He carefully takes out each urn and places them on the ground. He does the same with the box before shaking my hand.

"It's been a pleasure to meet you Rin, as I said earlier, I wish it were under better circumstances. If you ever need me, my card is in the envelope with your father's will."

"Thank you, Mr Myles."

"Anytime kid, look after yourself," he says as he gets back into his car. I don't move until his car is a tiny, blurry blot in the distance.

I turn away and head back to the tents, my mind already starting to figure out my next steps.

CHAPTER FIVE

1994 / 1995

In my first year alone, and by the first anniversary of everyone's deaths, I manage to rebuild four tents.

Rebuilding the tents was a lot trickier than I'd originally thought it was going to be. The tents were old, older than both me and my father, so the likelihood of getting like for like replacements is slim. And when Mr Myles looked for the shop that was meant to be located in Amwin Highstreet, he found it closed and awaiting demolition. The company has also shut down, so it's going to be impossible to get the exact same kind of fabric. Thankfully though, Mr Myles managed to find a fabric that was basically the same. He also got me a sewing kit. It was filled to the brim with different thickness of thread, proper fabric scissors and all the other sewing bits I could possibly need.

I've spent the last year cutting and patchworking the four smallest tents. I've also been cleaning out as much soot and dirt as possible from the original fabrics. It's been tricky to get out, the length of time that the soot has been sitting on the fabrics has let it absorb right into the fibres. I've got some of it out though, but the tents are going to be smelling like smoke for quite some time.

It's been hard, going through the tents, repairing them. Digging through the collapsed insides had me finding things that belonged the performers. The four small tents were once used by Alita, Harry, Tarron and Josie. Not a lot of their equipment survived the fires, all of their possessions and treasured items turned to ash. It was hard to see the remnants of their stuff, to remember that the last time they used it was the night of the fire. To honour them, I used some of the left over fabric trimmings to create name tags and attached them to the inside facing parts of the panel. *Name, Date of Birth, Date of Death, and Role.* It was the only way I could think to honour everyone without putting up gravestones. Gravestones which could be targeted and potentially destroyed if the people who did this found them.

I've also tended to the dead and burnt grass. I found a shovel in the back of the shed tent and used it to, essentially, scalp the ground. I worked on spreading as many grass seeds as possible to make the area as vibrant as possible. But when it wasn't working and the grass seeds refused to grow, I tried using the Circus magic. And it worked a little bit, tiny sections of grass started to grow. Unfortunately, I couldn't get much of the land done without feeling lightheaded and nauseous.

The magic was far more powerful than I had originally anticipated it to be. After even the slightest bit of use I come over with a splitting headache. It runs behind my eyes, down my neck and into my shoulders. It sometimes has the ability to render me immobile for a few hours. I haven't yet managed to understand how my father handled all of this. The excruciating pain makes me wonder if all of this is worth it. If all of this land and the tents are worth rebuilding at this point.

I confide in Mr Myles about this. I tell him about

my feelings, and he tells me not to worry. He tells me that everything will work out in the end. I just need to have patience.

So after taking a few days to work on a long term rebuild plan, I started restoration on the remaining tents. I manage to get them fixed slightly quicker, as this time round I know exactly what I'm doing. I repeat the same tributes on each tent, sewing the flaps of fabric to the inside corners.

Before I even think about rebuilding the internal structures of the tents, I take a break. During that break, I work on nurturing the magic. Moulding it and bending it to my will. It's a challenge, one that comes with many drawbacks. One of those being my lack of Mentor. The magic I have inside of me right now isn't really mine. Not yet at least. I cannot be called the master of my magic if I have not yet mastered it. So I work on mastering it. It takes me close to six months to take control of the magic inside of me. I make it work for me, but also with me. The magic has become me, has filled every single vein and muscle. The magic is a part of me and if I take care of it properly, then, in turn, it will take care of me.

When I restart the internal restoration of the tents, I use the magic to rebuild the beams and hang back up the string lights. I also use the magic to fix up the gangways. Most of them are showing signs of melting from the fire, but with a little summoning, I return to them their original glory. I don't overuse the magic though; I don't abuse the power I have been given. I use just enough that I can safely work and not injure myself with the heavy pieces of structure.

I manually replace all of the lightbulbs in each tent, and I make sure to renew the gas and electricity bills so that I can finally heat the family tent. Then I scrub every hard surface in both the show and activity tents, attempting to get the soot and smoky smell out of them.

A car rolls up outside of the tent. I place down my sponge and walk out of the tent.

"Hey Mr Myles."

"Hi Rin. Everything going okay?"

I nod, shaking my hands to get rid of the droplets of water and soap. "It's taking a while, but it's getting there."

"Good to see the tents looking refreshed. I must

say that I think I prefer them with patchwork."

"Thanks. It's a new era for the circus and I think the tents, and everything inside should reflect that."

"It's good to see you like this. I know it wasn't easy in the beginning, and it's probably not any easier now, but you're doing well. You should be proud of yourself. Oh and before I forget, I have something for you."

My eyes light up at the idea of what he brought me.

"Files?" I ask as he pulls out a large brown envelope.

"All six of them. Name, address, job, schedules, family, and so on. It's all in there and I hope it's helpful to you."

I take the envelope and stare at it.

The people who killed my family are going to pay for what they did. I'm *personally* going to make them pay for what they did. New senses of anger and righteousness run through my veins.

"Thank you, Mr Myles. This means *everything* to me."

"Anytime kid. I hope you get what you're

looking for. Contact me if you need anything else."

"I will. Thank you, Mr Myles, for everything you've done over the last two years."

"See you around kid," he says with a smile as he gets back into his car.

I walk back into the home tent, climb the stairs and head to my bedroom. I settle on the bed and tear open the envelope. I pull out all of the papers and scan over the information. Names, dates, routines of where they all drive, number plates, address, job, schedules and family. I smile to myself when I read that each one drives down Wesley Lane at least once a week.

A plan begins to form in my head. A plan that will cause them to suffer. A plan that will leave them feeling the pain that my family did before they died of their injuries. I will ensure that each one pays for what they did.

Six months. Six accidents.

"***Ronnie Alexander*** wrapped his car around a tree on Wesley Lane after driving home heavily under the influence of alcohol late Thursday evening. He was pronounced dead at the scene by paramedics who attempted to save him."

"***Amber Mitchells*** caused a head-on collision after swerving dangerously out of control on Wesley Lane in the early hours of Sunday morning. Emergency services managed to get her to the hospital where, unfortunately, she later died from her injuries."

"***Carter*** and ***Beth Vicotry***, husband and wife, were in the car that collided with Amber Mitchells on Sunday morning. Mr Vicotry was safely removed from the car and sent on his way to the hospital where he was later discharged with minor injuries. His wife, Beth Vicotry, was pronounced dead after attempts at the scene to revive her were unsuccessful."

"***Shelly Courts*** was hit by a police car on Wesley Lane on Monday afternoon. Dashcam footage given to the Independent Investigation Board showed that Miss Courts ran out into the road in pursuit of her dog. Miss Courts was rushed to hospital, but it's been reported that she has passed away from her injuries."

"***Andy Carlile*** rolled his car on Wesley Lane after a shocking twenty four hours of weather. Heavy rain and freezing temperatures turned the country road into an ice rink. Carlile was pronounced dead on arrival."

"***Carter Vicotry***, the sole survivor of the head on collision three months ago was killed this morning in the middle of Amwin town. It was reported that he stepped out in front of a bus. The bus driver says that Mr Vicotry came out of nowhere. Vicotry was pronounced dead on arrival."

"People in the Amwin area are beginning to wonder whether Wesley Lane is haunted. Over the last six months, six accidents have happened along the road behind me, and five people have died. The only survivor being Carter Vicotry, who, unfortunately passed away earlier this week after being hit by a bus. A lot of residents will remember the horrific deaths of The Circus Wonder Company, a much loved circus that was housed in the wood clearing on my left. Is this the work of vengeful spirits or is there more to these *accidents* that we just can't see? Back to you, Aila."

I turn away from the television set in the diner and clamber out of the booth feeling extremely satisfied.

Six murderers.

Six *dead* murderers.

All of them have gotten what they deserve, and a deep sense of satisfaction settles inside of me.

I step onto the pavement, taking in the sunshine and the new sense of freedom I feel knowing that justice has been served.

When I reach Wesley Lane, I cut into the forest. I follow one of the many trekking paths all the way to the clearing. As I reach the outer tents, I feel my heart speed up and pins and needles develop over my heart. Pain envelopes me and my chest tightens as I collapse to my knees. My back spasms and I fall forwards, my hands hitting the ground. I groan as a second wave of pain tears through me, and my hands come up to my shirt. I grab it round the fabric in the middle and I rip it open. The buttons from my shirt fly everywhere and I move the fabric away from my chest. The veins on my chest, specifically the veins over my heart, are turning black. They're faint, but I can see them growing, tracking along my skin. I groan again as the pain over my heart intensifies.

I can't move as the heavens open, and the rain starts to pour. All I can do is let myself fall onto my back, my shirt still open, my bare chest facing the sky. The veins continue to grow, to twinge and ache. The rain soaks me head to toe, my clothes becoming heavy with water and caked in mud.

Magic will always have consequences, that's something my father's Mentor always told him. I heard him repeat over and over, so I can safely assume that this is my punishment, or the beginning of a warning. A warning to use the magic very carefully.

CHAPTER SIX

1996 / 1997

Finishing off the final touches on the circus is like a weight being lifted from my shoulders.

It's taken two years to rebuild every single tent and structure. Six months to master, and fully understand, the magic that lies within me. I'm still working on controlling the magic, I might have mastered it in those six months, but it has taken, and will continue to take, a lot longer to learn how to control it.

It's New Year's Day today, the first of January. The beginning of the third year since the incident. By now, everyone in Amwin has moved on. It's been three years, there's no reason for everyone to continue being wary about what happened that night. Besides, the people who did it are dead, I made sure of that.

But moving on is a luxury that I don't get.

I'm determined to make sure that my father's legacy will be remembered, this circus will come back to life and will captivate audiences again and again. The only thing missing at the moment is the performers, so I spend an evening at the local diner. I wine and dine the local talent scouts and the Level 6 Performing Arts students. I ask them whether they would like to audition for a job that will be waiting for them as soon as they graduate. I get asked a lot of questions about The Circus Wonder. About the incident three years ago, and about the safety of the circus. I reassure each and every person that the circus is safe, and I will ensure that it remains that way. The night turns out to be a success as I manage to get a number of students to sign up for the initial round of auditions.

As I tidy up the papers I brought with me, a girl sits herself down on the chair opposite me.

I glance up at her curiously.

"Hello?"

"Hi, I'm Willow Osley," she says, sticking out her hand for me to shake.

I nod and shake her hand. "Are you here to sign up for the auditions?"

"No."

"Did you want information about a career after graduation?"

"No."

I pull a face, one a mixture of confusion and disinterest. "What can I do for you then?"

"I read what happened to your family. It wasn't announced if they ever found you, but I saw you in the clearing. I saw you patching the roofs and scrubbing every scrubbable surface."

My mood instantly sours, more than it had already for her not having an actual reason for coming over here. No one should've been lurking in the woods around the circus clearing. It's private land. Land owned by the Masters family.

"I think it would be best if you leave," I say, a warning laced in my tone.

She shakes her head. "I needed to speak to you. My father brought me to The Circus Wonder a lot. He worked in the ticket booths, welcoming guests. He didn't die in the fire as he lived at home with me."

My brain clicks. The Osley surname sounded familiar. Jack Osley, a lovely man who made conversation with just about every guest whoever passed through the gates. I let my face relax and lean back in my chair.

"I remember him. He would always ask me about the acts and when my father was going to let me host a show as the Ringmaster. Jack was a good man; he was the one to–to discover my sister Riya in the lake. He jumped in without regard to his own saf-safety," I say, stuttering at the memory.

Willow smiles sadly at me as she reaches across the table and grabs my hand. She squeezes it. "He told me he'd do it over and over again if it meant that your family got that five extra minutes with her."

"I'm sorry I was rude to you before."

She shakes her head. "There's no need to apologise. I understand you being wary of people, especially when they sit down at your table uninvited."

I smile.

"Do you remember me? I know you probably met thousands of guests, but I was always there."

"I think I do. If I'm right in thinking, then I believe I found you hiding behind the main tent. You'd stolen a couple of packets of sweets from one of the vendor carts and were hiding with them."

She laughs and jumps slightly in her seat. "That was me. I can't believe you remembered that."

"Pretty hard not to after I joined you and then we were chased by the vendor who owned the sweets."

We reminisce some more. Laughing and joking about our time at The Circus Wonder. I tell her stories about things that happened behind the scenes, stories about things that happened in rehearsals or overnight. She then tells me about the other mischief that she got up to whenever she visited. It feels nice to laugh again, to properly laugh. To feel joy and happiness when I think of my family instead of having the memories of their final moments jump to the forefront of my mind.

"Willow?" I ask as we stop laughing.

"Yes?"

"Will you help me with the auditions? Like when it comes to choosing the acts? You know how the circus used to be, and I want the circus to become more than it was. Better, improved. Subtle with magic and with the focus on talented acts."

She smiles at me. "Of course I'll help you. When do you want to start auditions?"

"In three days."

"I'll be there."

We bond over our love of the seaside and circuses. We drink and laugh and have fun, more fun than I think I've had in years. We continue to talk until we're kicked out of the diner at closing. And when we step out of the diner, we're more than a little drunk as we stumble back to the clearing before falling into bed together. Willow stays until mid-morning the next day. I cook us breakfast, and by cook I mean putting a couple of pieces of bread in the toaster, before I walk her to Wesley Lane. She promises to come back in two days' time to help with auditions, and she does exactly that.

Together we set up the main tent for the auditions. We set up three tables, two of them next to each other just off centre in the performance ring. The third one is placed by the entrance for people to sign in on. We also set up the bleachers so that anyone auditioning can sit and watch if they want to, both before and after their audition.

The day passes quickly, and before I know it Willow and I are tucked up in my bed again. I'm leaning against the headboard with my right arm around Willow's shoulders.

"What if I helped you with the circus?"

"What do you mean?" I ask. She shuffles so that she's looking me in the eyes.

"What if I helped you with the maintenance and upkeep?"

"You don't need to do that. I've got all of the maintenance under control."

"I know you do. You've done so well to revamp the whole place and take care of it on your own, but I want to help you. I know our time together hasn't reached over a week yet, but I want to help you. I want to work here, at the circus."

"I think I'd like that; it does get lonely sometimes. There's no one to talk to, other than myself. Well, I do have Mr Myles, but he has a job during the week, so he doesn't visit unless I need him to," I tell her. Her hand traces over my bare chest, her fingernails narrowly missing the black veins tracking away from my heart. She doesn't ask about them, nor does she accidentally touch them. I can tell she's curious though, and one day I'll tell her about them.

"I'm happy to keep you company. If I'm honest, I've been looking for a reason to quit my job. I hate my manager. I hate how stuffy the shop is and how bitchy some of the customers are. I'd be more than happy to quit and move here, to work here and help you."

I nod, debating it. Would it be so bad to have company here? To have someone to talk to every day. Someone to be my friend?

"Is that something you're sure you want? I don't have a lot to offer you. The money my father left me is meant to cover me for the rest of my life, but I don't want to overuse it. Until the circus is properly up and running, life will be pretty boring," I explain to her, not wanting Willow to make a hasty decision now that she might come to regret in the future.

"Rin, I know there's not a lot to offer, and I'm not here for the money your father left you. That's yours and yours alone. I have my own money that

I've been saving and, if you let me help you and stay here, I'll move out of my flat. I want to be here with you Rin. I want to be in the place my father loved and be in the place that is full of magic."

I smile at her, at her sincerity and love that she uses when she speaks of the circus. The arm I've draped around her shoulders pulls her to me closer and her hand gently rests on the black veins.

"I guess I have a lot to tell you then," I say, referring to the actual magic that resides within the circus.

※

For four weeks, we watch countless first auditions for our background acts and our vendors. Willow went through all of the information I'd gathered at the diner the other night. She carefully picked through the information and called everyone she thought could be a good fit for the circus.

We go through four rounds of auditions in total. Each group of ten candidates gets a week worth of auditions, and at the end of each day, we eliminate two candidates. We do that until we are left with 10 candidates. We test the group's chemistry, and it takes us just under two weeks to settle on the group. We interchange two candidates with two candidates that we sent home because of conflicting personalities, but by the final Friday, we finalised our group of ten background acts. We also take on three vendors who applied via an ad I placed in the local diner.

I give them a guided tour. I show them where all the facilities that they'll be using are when they're here. I've since learnt from the incident to not have as many cast members living on site, but it will be an option available to them.

"Any questions?" I ask as I lead the tour back to the main tent.

"With the utmost respect to those who came before us, but I must ask if you would consider this place to be haunted?" Mina, my new fortune teller, asks.

"I believe that the souls of my family reside here, they rest here. But I believe that they have no ill intentions toward those who respect the circus and the way it works. Willow, the lovely girl you met earlier, helped me create a resting place worthy of those who died. You are all safe here, *you* are the future of The

Circus Wonder, and those whose footsteps you follow in will respect that."

"Thank you," she says with a bow of her head.

From that day, and after sorting out where everyone wants to stay, we dive straight into rehearsals. We start the training required for some of the acts before we begin to properly rebuild The Circus Wonder.

It takes eight weeks of training to building up their knowledge and techniques which then leads into four months of proper rehearsals. The proper rehearsals allow us start to building their routines, to build their characters and their personas. The rehearsals are tough and long. We start early in the morning and finish in the late evening, but it's all worth it when we are able to start putting the final touches on their acts.

Willow and I have been busy in the evenings when the performers have left. We spend hours looking through potential costume designs. We sketch some of our own and we go shopping for fabrics and accessories. We call it a night at about half ten every evening, it gives us enough time after everyone leaves to get the tasks that need to be done, finished before we start working again the next morning.

Keeping busy all day everyday helps take my mind off the little bits of guilt that keep pulling at my chest. *I replaced them*, my mind keeps telling me. Thoughts like those plague my mind day in and day out, making it hard to focus on the performers who need me. Every day I try to reassure myself that people will come and watch the Circus. Fans from the past will return to the clearing and they will love the performers, the show, the atmosphere. But at the same time, I have to remind myself that people may forget about those who came before them. New fans will only remember this round of performers, and my family will slip into the background, dead and forgotten.

"Hey, what are you thinking so hard about?" Willow asks as she sits next to me, one of her hands grasping one of mine.

"Everything," I say honestly.

She presses a kiss to my temple before resting her head on my shoulder. "Missing them?"

"Yeah, just a little." Tears sting my eyes and I try

to blink them away before she can see them fall. We've grown very close over the last six months and just like our meeting, our sort of– and unconfirmed– relationship has been the best thing to happen to me in a while. She's kept me grounded, she's helped with keeping my head in the game and not letting the negative thoughts get to me. I'm so grateful for Willow. She's been my rock throughout this entire process, and I think it's safe to say I love her.

"Three and a half years today, right?"

I nod.

"I know today is hard for you, but I think I have something that will cheer you up."

I turn to her. "What is it?"

"I know we've not been together long, and this is probably one of the last things either of us need right now but…" She pauses.

"But?"

"I'm pregnant," she blurts out, holding eye contact with me and looking hopeful.

I blink a few times, shocked. "Pregnant?"

"Uh-huh. Are you happy?" She looks at me with tears forming in her eyes. It takes me a moment, but I smile widely at her.

"Happier than ever," I say as I stand up from the bed and pull her to me. I cup her cheeks and kiss her. When we pull away I pick her up and spin her around. We both laugh and when I put her down, I kiss her again.

"I'm so happy," she murmurs.

"Me too. I love you, Willow. So much so that I don't think I have enough words."

Life over the last three and a half years has had its ups and downs, certainly more downs than ups but it feels like things are finally beginning to look up.

CHAPTER SEVEN

1998 / 2002 / 2006

On the 5th of April 1997, Willow gave birth to our babies.

Our relationship only grew stronger after she told me she was pregnant. We worked on establishing our relationship. We tried labelling ourselves as boyfriend and girlfriend, but it didn't feel right. That label felt premature, felt that we maybe weren't really serious about each other despite knowing how we felt about each other. I thought about getting married, but Willow scowled at the idea. She said she didn't think that marriage was us, it didn't capture what we were. We weren't looking for a way to secure our babies or life together. We'd already decided to spend the rest of our lives with each other. We feel like our souls are intertwined, everything in our lives is wrapped around the other. We're comfortable and safe with each other that giving our relationship a title would seem superficial, it would take away from us as a pair and us as people.

Despite being pregnant, Willow didn't slow down until a few hours before going into labour. She refused to sit still and together we brought The Circus Wonder back to life. Not only did we achieve a successful relaunch, but we've also secured investors. Some of the money my father left me, before I knew any money had been left to me, was used to return previous investors' money. We're in a good place financially, living in a safe place and more in love than ever. We've been inseparable, in fact, since the twins were born we've hardly left each other's sides.

But as strong as our love is, the way we've grown together and brought The Circus Wonder back to life is a testament to how strong we are. I'm not the same person I was a year ago. The black veins tracking from my heart have gotten darker, and I can feel the magic far more than ever before. It's growing, gathering energy and I worry that at some point I will no longer be the master of my own magic, that it will turn on me and become *my* master. It's been keeping me up at night, the pain in my chest and the whispers in my head can't be ignored.

"Enna," the voice says, repeating the name for the fourth time today. I don't know what it means. Is Enna a person? An object? An artefact, perhaps? It's unclear and distracting, and it's taking my focus away from my children on their birthday.

We're having a small celebration in the main tent. The Circus Wonder has become like a little family again. The twins' birth really helped with that.

"Happy birthday to youuuuu," everyone sings before clapping as the twins attempt to blow out the candles on their birthday muffins.

I bend down and pick up Rosain, resting him on my hip before bending back down and collecting Rowyna and settling on my other hip. Willow sorts their birthday muffins into two bowls as I place them in their highchairs.

"Enna," the voice hisses.

My head snaps up and my eyes dart around the tent.

"Rin, you okay?" Willow asks, one of her hands

brushing my bicep.

It takes me a second to come back to myself, but I nod. "Yes, sorry. Thought I heard something."

She nods and goes back to fussing over the twins. While she is distracted, I sneak off, rounding the edge of the crowd. I reach the entrance to the tent just as the pain around my heart starts again and nausea starts to rise up my throat. I make it far enough away that no one will hear me as I throw up. I cough and retch. The pain is like nothing I've felt before, and I fear that the magic may be getting too much for me. I feel marginally better once the sickness passes, but the tightness in my chest has me remaining breathless.

"Rin?"

I turn and see Mr Myles walking toward me.

"Mr Myles. It's been a while," I say as we shake hands.

"Everything alright? You look rather pale for someone celebrating their kids' first birthday."

I frown. "How do you know it's their birthday?"

"Son, I know everything that goes on in this circus. And Willow sent me an invite. Though I figured I could also use the opportunity to check on things, hope I'm not stepping on your toes."

I shake my head. "No, you're good. And it turns out you're exactly the person I needed to see today. I have some questions I'd like to ask you."

He nods and takes a seat on one of the wooden benches I placed around the site. "Hit me with them."

I nod and join him on the bench. "Did my father ever tell you about the magic he used? And did he ever mention hearing voices?"

"Your father gave me a book about the magic he was using. It was given to him by his Mentor, and he gave me strict instructions not to give it to you unless I thought it was absolutely necessary. Which I think now might be the time." He pulls a book out of the inner pocket of his blazer and hands it to me. "One of the symptoms listed in this book, for people who have used the magic for three and a half to four years, is that the wielder develops an affinity for hearing voices. But the voices aren't meant to be bad, they're an aid."

"What kind of aid?"

"Guidance. Assistance. You're bound to gain enemies just like your father did. The difference is that you will be able to tell if people are going to be harmful and passive. The magic will help you gauge the safety measures you'll need to take in order to protect everyone. Your magic is linked with, not only your fate, but the fate of those who will end up here in the Circus."

"I can keep my family safe?"

"You can do much more than just keep them safe Rin, you can detect the slightest shift in people's intentions toward the circus. You will be able to foresee an attack before it even happens. All of this is in the book."

I nod. "Thank you, Mr Myles. Could you do some digging for me?"

"Of course. What do you need me to check?"

"The voice keeps saying Enna, and I have no idea what or who Enna is."

He nods. "I think the magic is trying to warn you about Enna Stradan. 16 years old and extremely curious about the deaths on Wesley Lane. She's a bright kid, but if she continues to explore the story then she has the potential to become a threat."

Enna Stradan. It makes sense. Enna Stradan

could be a problem, a *threat* to all I have built. I cannot allow that to happen, I won't have everything taken away from me for a second time.

"You think she knows it was me?"

"No. Her article is very much in the research stage. The only reason I know about it is because she's been very vocal with my assistant about trying to interview me. I've been refusing, of course, those deaths are for us, and us alone, to know about."

I nod. "What would you suggest I do?"

"Get rid of her. Or keep her."

I scoff. "How would I keep her?"

He taps the front cover of the book. "All of the information is in there. That's the best way for you to learn what you need to do to secure yourself and your family."

"Thank you, Mr Myles," I say as we shake hands.

"No need to thank me, Rin. Just let me grab a slice of cake before I head out."

I shake my head laughing, and gesture to the tent. I watch him leave before having a quick flick through the book. Everything I could possibly need is in here, and I know exactly what I will be doing once everyone is asleep.

※

When I'm sure that Willow is asleep, I carefully get out of bed and make my way down to the outer edges of the property.

While Willow was sorting out the twins' bottles earlier, I had a flick through some of the pages and came across a section for protections. I skim read through most of them and folded the corners of the pages that I could use. I quickly open the book and flick to the folded corner. A page containing a protection spell that will keep both the magic and those I decide to *keep* inside the circus protected. I will also use it to distort the memories of those who enter as a way of keeping the magic and those I *keep,* out of my visitors' memories. The only memories they will leave the circus with are those of joy.

I bend down and start drawing the circle of protection around the site. I use a piece of what I believe to be chalk, to draw the circle. It was attached to the back page of the book with other pieces of metal and shapes which I assume will help with other spells in the book. Every ten steps the book tells me to draw a symbol. I carefully draw each symbol, and after the better part of an hour, I finally finish the protection circle. I skim over the instructions again and see that I need to head to the very centre of the land and draw one final symbol. A symbol that will link everything together and will activate the protection. I say the words written at the bottom of the instructions as I draw the symbol.

"Tiwh esthe bolsyms, Eh esocheo oreptec ym leople. Orefereve arugd su, enerv elt setoh tiwh lli wlil chera su."

"With these symbols, I choose to protect my people. Forever guard us, never let those with ill will reach us."

The markings glow red before disappearing into the soil. I can vaguely see the protection around the edge of the land. It makes me feel better a lot better. *A lot safer.* Everyone who is part of The Circus Wonder will be safe, alongside Mr Myles, and those with ill intentions won't make it very far before they forget their intentions. This is the only way to keep my family safe and I won't let the same thing happen again.

"I can't let it happen again," I murmur to myself as I pull out my mobile phone. I select Mr Myles's number and I bring the phone to my ear, letting it ring.

"Rin? Is everything okay?" he asks with a worried tone.

"Everything is fine. I just wanted to let you know that the book has been very helpful. I've put a protection around the land."

"I'm glad. Is there something else you need my help with?"

"Yes, actually. I want you to get Enna down to the circus under false pretences. I'll deal with her after that."

"Copy. Is that all?"

"Yes, thank you. Goodbye," I say as I hang up.

That phone call ended up changing a lot for me. Enna is the first. She comes to me under the illusion that I will be answering her questions, that I will be giving her material for her journalism article. Instead I give her a mark. A mark that will bring her back to me twenty four hours after the initial transfer. Her mind will become scrambled, and she will be under the impression that she was always meant to end up in The Circus Wonder. That she's *always* been with us. And once she returns, fully under the influence of my magic, I welcome her with open arms. I take her on a tour and show her the ropes. She becomes my priority, the first member of the main cast. No one in the family asks questions since I'm honest about what is happening. I'm up front with them and let them know that they are, and always will be, protected.

Once people notice she's gone, missing posters start to go up. But it's no use. No one knows where she's gone and those who come visit the circus don't know that they're looking right at her.

But Enna isn't the only one who disappears and joins the circus. In 2002, Arjun Orion becomes the second main cast member. Mr Myles heard about someone poking and prodding at the strange deaths of my family and the other deaths that occurred in the area. I was warned about him and made sure to deal with him swiftly, just like Enna. After letting him settle in, I've come to find that he's quite similar to Enna. Both of them were studying journalism with the hopes of becoming trainee journalists and researchers. But now he's mine, and his missing posters eventually fall to the ground in a mess of ripped and faded paper.

Arjun thrills my audience. He captivates regulars and newcomers with his dazzling routine. He holds everyone's attention and quickly becomes a household name. Well, his circus persona becomes a household name, The Fire King. The way he manipulates the flames keeps the audience thoroughly entertained and leaves me extremely pleased with him. He reminds a little bit of Alfie, but unlike Arjun, Alfie couldn't quite work the flames the same way.

Then, in 2006, after I find him digging through the bins behind the outer tents, Knox Lewis joins my circus, completely of his own free will. He takes on the role of the Jester. He makes my audiences clutch at their stomachs with laughter as he tells jokes and performs his act. He's talented, naturally so to the point where I didn't need to interfere with my magic. He's quickly become a fan favourite for the pre-show warm up.

My main performers are the true stars of the show. They've merged in well with the background acts and bring a certain finesse to the shows. I couldn't be happier with how everything has turned out, but sometimes I wonder if there may have been a better way to deal with them. A better way than kidnapping them. Those thoughts alone lead me down a rabbit hole of doubt and worry.

Am I worried about people figuring out what's going on? Not really. The people in this town haven't noticed what is happening right under their noses, although my magic is mostly responsible for that.

Am I worried that the use of my magic is slowly turning me into something other than the guy who rebuilt his home? A little. I worry about my children and my Willow. I worry that my magic will change me, that I will become a completely different person to the person that Willow fell in love with. But at the same time, I feel that as long as I have them, the darkness will never be able to take over completely. I can stave off the darkness as long as I have them in my life, as long as I love them, and they love me.

But there's one thought that scares me the most.

A thought about something that I have no control over. The thought that every four years, the magic will whisper to me. It will whine at me and cause extremely painful migraines until I obey and take the next person. I have no control over that part anymore, over that voice. I just pray that this is something that will eventually go away.

CHAPTER EIGHT

2010 / 2014 / 2018

Internationally touring with the Circus is the ultimate goal.

And tonight is The Circus Wonder's reintroduction to the world, in Paris, France. A crowd of over five thousand people have come to witness the great name that The Circus Wonder, mark two, has made for itself.

After selling out shows all around the United Kingdom, we've finally made it to another country. We are welcomed with banners and open arms by French fans as we make our way to the performance ground. We don't have the tents with us for this trip, they're being looked and protected after by Mr Myles. Our performances in Paris are open air ones, so our tents wouldn't have been needed anyway.

"Rin, this place is beautiful," Willow gushes. She curls herself into my side as we walk around our performance space.

"I know, I can't believe we get to perform here."

"This is all because of you. *You* made the circus successful again."

"I couldn't have done this without you," I say, leaning my head down to kiss her.

"Ewwww, please stop," Rowyna groans as she walks past us. Willow and I laugh and watch her roll her eyes. While Willow and I haven't gotten married, our relationship hasn't wavered in the amount of love, adoration and dedication we have toward each other. I love Willow with all my heart, and I know she feels the same. We don't need to get married to prove our love for each other.

"Does love disgust you, Rowyna?" I ask her.

"It does when it's you two. It's scary for any child to witness their parents practically climb on top of each other in the middle of the street."

I shake my head playfully at her as my mind flashes back to one of the last conversations I had with Rayna. In that conversation she said something similar, and it occurs to me just how similar Rowyna is to her aunt.

"Right, warm up time," Enna says, gathering all of the performers while Willow and I move to make sure the rest of the show's elements have been set up correctly.

The atmosphere around me fizzles with excitement as the crowds start to pour in.

I stand and watch from the middle of my ring. My magic seems to respond to the electric atmosphere as I feel it rush through my veins. I've never felt like this before, not even in the shows back home. I feel light and airy and bounce on the balls of my feet as I wait for the audience to settle. As the lights around me flash and flicker, the signal that the show is about to start, I welcome the audience. I introduce them to the circus before we begin the entertainment. I guide them through the starting acts, the card tricks, the dancing and the basic illusions before leading them into the best, and if I do say so myself, the best part.

I take them through Enna's dance. Her ability to dance between the lights and the manipulation of the lights around her as they reflect off her costume. The streams of light appear to almost dance with her. They become her partner, they become her guide. She works seamlessly with the light that you could hear a pin drop. The audience sits there in sheer silence as they admire her act, only making a sound when they give her a standing ovation at the end.

Arjun is up next and if the audience loved Enna then they seem to be entranced by him, completely captivated with his act. He plays with fire, lighting hoops before flinging them up into the air and catching them in a precarious stack. He has the audience *oohing* and *ahhing* at the sheer skill he presents. He calls an audience member to the stage and has them stand in the middle of a hoop. A hoop he then sets on fire. He pulls it up and over the guy's head. The fire seems to be attracted to the man as it eats away at his clothes only to turn them into a suit so fancy you'd think he was a CEO.

The audience applauds, simply stunned at what they have witnessed.

Knox's act comes and goes, making the audience double over with laughter before it seamlessly transitions into Rosain's aerial act. Over the last year or so, he's taken quite an interest in aerial work, so I asked him if he wanted to become an aerial artist. He said he did, so I started training him. He's proved to be quite talented, naturally so, and he asked if he could perform at the Paris show. I agreed.

He waltzes across the stage and circles the outside.

"I need a volunteer," he announces as his eyes lock on a blonde-haired girl. He steps up onto the edge and holds his hand out to her. She hesitates but quickly places her hand in his to cover up her uncertainty.

Ro helps her over the railing and down onto the stage. He guides her to stand on the grey X in the middle of the stage. He tells the audience what he's going to do before he seats himself upside down on his hoop. He reaches down, grabs onto her hands and pulls her up with him. They spin a little and she laughs, which makes Ro smile. A genuine smile that I've only ever seen him use with his sister.

The whole act is like a sensual dance. Ro pulls the girl up onto his lap as he sits up properly inside of his hoop. He says something to her which makes her nod before he slides off and catches her mid fall. They spin and flip and move together like plumes of smoke dancing in the wind. It's enchanting to watch and I find myself lost in the act, just like the audience are. I hadn't expected his first show to turn out quite like this, but my son has some serious talent. Talent which I will be adding to the shows permanently if that is something he's willing to do. At the end of the routine, he places the girl back on solid ground before they both bow. She says something to him before heading back into the crowd.

"Veve Winston," the voice chirps and I have to take a deep breath as I step onto the stage.

Not now, I think to myself as I turn to face the audience.

"Thank you to everyone who came out to watch our international debut. We'll be back tomorrow night before moving on to the next stops in our international tour."

The audience claps and hoots as everyone comes out to take their bows.

"Veve Winston."

"Veve Winston."

"VEVE Winston."

"VEVE WINSTON."

I make a beeline for the seat that the blonde girl was sitting in. She must clock me coming toward me as she takes a few steps down onto the stage.

"Hi, I just wanted to say thank you for the chance to come on stage tonight. It was magical," she blurts out, her voice thick with a French accent.

I smile at her. "It was all on my son. I'm Rin Masters, the owner of this fine circus." I extend my hand, a gesture for us to shake hands. She takes my hand, shaking it briefly and I feel the transfer happen. I feel my magic seep from my hand onto hers. I don't mean for it to happen, taking this girl from here doesn't sit right. She has done nothing to me, but for some reason the magic has taken over me. It has forced the mark to transfer to this girl without my say so and that is something I am going to have to work out how to fix.

"Well, it was amazing regardless. I'm Veve Winston, by the way."

"It was nice to meet you, Veve," I say with a

smile before turning my back to her. I walk away, knowing that Veve will be coming back to England with me, whether I like it or not.

Our second and final performance in Paris goes on without a hitch. This audience loves it, maybe even more so than last night. The show passes by quickly and before anyone knows it, we're loading ourselves onto a ferry to get back to Dover. As I check in last with the guard, I hear shouting behind me. I turn and see Veve running toward us, pulling a suitcase.

"Mr Masters. Oh, Mr Masters," she calls.

"Veve?"

"Yes. Oh mon dieu, that was a long run. Mr Masters, please take me with you. Please let me play as part of your troupe."

I smile at her, knowing that, technically, she's coming regardless of my next words. But to keep the magic at bay, and to ease my own mind, I ask her a question. "Are your parents okay with this?"

"They're fine with it. Please, please take me with you."

That's all I need to hear before I welcome Veve to her new family. A family that will care for her no matter what. I lead introductions, letting her meet everyone before we all settle down for a brief sleep before we arrive back home.

I settle down next to Willow, we've commandeered the first of many dining areas on the ferry. It's been booked out completely so that only myself, my family and the circus members are permitted to enter. I wrap an arm around Willow's shoulder as we watch Rosain and Veve. They settle next to each other and seem content as they mutter to one another.

"Goodnight my love," I whisper against Willow's head as she settles against me, closing her eyes.

For once, the voice has quieted down quite quickly. It seems to be satisfied with the quick resolution to its wanting of Veve. Again, I pray that she is the last, but a crushing pain has me struggling to remain still. I carefully peek at my chest, being careful not to disturb Willow, and see that the dark veins have spread out further, they're almost reaching the bottom of my ribs. The veins at the top of my chest are close to stretching over my shoulder. A reminder of what I have been doing, of what the magic is *making* me do.

I look up and see Rosain's eyes fixed on my chest. He looks me in the eyes knowingly. I shake my head, a subtle warning for him not to ask questions. I don't have a cure for this, nor do I want to tell my son about the darker and poisonous side of the magic I use in our home. One day I will tell him, but today is not that day. By the time I tell him and Rowyna what this is, they'll have had enough time to choose whether or not they want to be a part of the circus's future. And while none of us appear to age while we are safely within the confines of the magic, I want my children to have the choice to escape, to leave and live a normal life. I won't let this magic trap them and I won't let it take them without their permission.

Over the next eight years, the veins only get worse, and the voice only gets stronger. It demands more and in the end, Felix Reed and Ara True join us.

They take up their places in the circus as our illusionist slash clairvoyant, and our living doll slash music box act. The people of Amwin still haven't realised what has been happening right under their noses. That their people have been going missing and reappearing on a piece of land not even ten minutes from the town centre. The magic wielder part of me is glad that my magic is working so well, that it's keeping the memories distorted and my performers safe, but the human part of me is tired. It wishes that someone would realise what is going on. I wish someone would save me and say they'll take on the magic. I could give up everything and live a quiet life with Willow. But I can't. So, I make my protections stronger.

I take steps to secure my magic to ensure that chaos does not leave the confines of the circus line, because after delving deeper into the history of this magic, it requires the user to have as many people around them as possible. Enough people to be able to ensure enough bodies are present for it to control. It feeds off their life forces, it locks into the people I have around me all the time. It tethers them to me. But thankfully, it only works on those who perform, those who have no blood relation to me which means Rosain and Rowyna are safe. Willow is safe too after I made it clear she was off limits.

Although, it has recently dawned on me that I don't know why my father wanted me to take this on, to become what he would have eventually. But what I can say I know is that he had no idea what he was dealing with, and that I have barely scratched the surface.

CHAPTER NINE

October 2020

My forty - third birthday is everything I wanted and more.

Willow surprises me with breakfast in bed, before telling me that Rosain and Rowyna have agreed to take over Ringmaster duties today. They've both been showing a great interest in the role, so I've been training them up. It also gives me the chance to consider letting them take over completely, so that I can spend time with Willow while I still have control of the magic, instead of it having control of me. Giving the magic over to them is one of the last things I will do if they take over. I hope that by splitting it between them, it won't be nearly as toxic and toll-taking on their bodies and minds as it has been on mine.

"Come on, there's someone who wants to talk to you," Willow says as she drags me toward the main tent.

"Wills, you said we'd just relax today. No meetings or directing."

She stops and steps so that our chests are touching. "I know but I promise this is the only one. Then we can go back and relax."

I smile at her and kiss her forehead. "Okay. Who is this person?"

"Someone from a place far, far, away."

I laugh. "Seriously?"

"Yes."

Inside the main tent, a man in Victorian style clothes stands with his arms crossed over his chest. He looks extremely out of place as he observes his surroundings.

"Good morning," I say, drawing his attention.

"Good morning. Are you Mr Masters?" he asks.

I nod and step forward, offering my hand. "I am. Who are you?"

"I am Simion Witzal of the Kazilli Royal family, and I have come to ask if you and your Circus would be willing to come and perform in my country."

"Your country? Kazilli isn't a country here."

He nods. "Kazil isn't a country *here*, you're right. But it is in my reality, and we are in the process of trying to sign a deal with another country. We are holding an entertainment showcase on the night we plan to get them to sign the deal, and we've heard stories about The Circus Wonder."

I raise my eyebrow. "You've heard of us?"

"Yes. Stories of your great performances have slipped through the cracks and repeated back to me. I had to come witness your work for myself, but I'd like to informally extend the opportunity to come and perform in the palace."

I'm stunned, and suspicious. While the book containing all magic information had a brief section on other worlds and how they can be accessed, I never thought that they would know about The Circus Wonder. Compared to a lot of things, I feel that we would've been the last thing they'd hear about.

"I understand your hesitancy. I know that this is an unexpected visit, but I assure you there is nothing hidden inside of my offer. I'm the one in charge of the acts and anything to do with performing at the palace goes through myself and myself alone. You needn't be worried about anything bad happening as security teams will be provided."

"Well, you're more than welcome to come to the show tonight. My children, Rosain and Rowyna, are the ones running things at the moment. They are both in training to take over from me at some point so if it's alright with you, they'll be leading tonight's performance."

"I don't mind at all. And if it's okay with you, I'd like to just hang around here until the performance. I don't know the area at all, and I'd rather not find myself in any trouble."

"Fine by me. Everyone will be in for rehearsals soon, so feel free to watch."

"Thank you, Mr Masters."

"You're welcome, now if you'll excuse us, we have something to attend to," I say before dragging Willow away and back to our bedroom for a relaxing afternoon.

Willow and spent the rest of the afternoon cuddled up

in bed and watching tv. A totally lazy day, something we haven't had for a while.

But now, we're sitting in the crowds in the main tent. Mr Witzal is sitting next to us and appears to be enjoying the show. He's completely enraptured by what's happening in the Ring that I can just enjoy the show as well. I don't need to talk him through everything that's happening, so I have the chance to enjoy the show that I've been a part of for so long. To see what the audience sees when they watch it.

"I'm glad you're letting them take on more responsibility, I know it's been taking a toll on you," Willow says lowly in my ear as her hand presses against my heart. She's seen the veins, the tracking of the darkness as it spreads, but it has slowed down since I started sharing the circus with the twins. I think it comforts her that I'm letting the twins take on more responsibility, and I think it gives her a small amount of peace knowing that I'm not going to be killed by the magic coursing through me.

"So am I. I want to spend as much time as possible with you."

The performance passes by a lot quicker than I

want it to. I wanted to spend more time watching, more time feeling immersed in everything The Circus Wonder has to offer. But it was like as soon as the action started, it ended. An emptiness settles inside of me and I'm desperate to watch it all over again.

"Well done you two," I say as I hug Ro and Rowyna. "That was spectacular."

"Thanks dad," they mutter, clearly embarrassed by being given praise by their father.

"I would like to introduce you to Mr Witzal, he's a representative from the Royal Family of Kazil and is actively looking for acts to perform at a showcase they are hosting. Mr Witzal, this Rosain and Rowyna."

"Thank you, Mr Masters. It's a pleasure to meet both of you, and I'd like to start by saying what a fantastic show you put on tonight. I'd like to officially invite you to come and perform for the Kazilli Royal family."

"Thank you, Mr Witzal, but our father should really make the decision about where we perform," Rowyna says politely before looking up at me.

"Actually, I've been thinking about this, and I've

decided that you two should make this decision. I want to give you two more independence with the Circus in its entirety. The decision is yours," I tell them. They both nod, looking a little scared but they seem not to let it get to them as they turn back to Mr Witzal.

"Thank you for the offer, Mr Witzal," Rosain says. "We would love to perform for your Royal family."

Witzal claps and smiles. "Perfect. I'll be back in a few days to collect you. There's nothing you guys need to do other than pack the outfits you'll need. A stage and other necessities will be provided during your stay."

"Thank you, Mr Witzal," Rowyna says as she shakes hands with him before the two of them walk away.

"Looks like we're going on another adventure. I hope that the twins can take this on," Willow says as she hugs my side.

"Looks like it. I believe that they will do this successfully, it'll just be like running the evenings here. They'll be okay, and if they need me, I'll be close by."

※

After a successful show in Kazil, we are offered the chance to tour the rest of the reality.

We perform in Altaine, Bordova, Tibori, Madoneia, Pabria and the Corvian Republic. In each country we are showered with love and excited audiences who beg for us to return, to which we tell them one day. One day we'll be back to entertain them again.

After six months of touring these countries, I decide it's time for Rosain and Rowyna to take over completely. For them to become the Ringmaster and Ringmistress. I have them initiated. I let them take on the responsibilities, but I have yet to give them the magic. I need more time to figure out how to transfer it to them, but when I do, they will become the most powerful people in the world, and the best entertainers anyone has ever seen.

A Circus of Wonder

A. Carys

A Circus of Wonder

NOW, 2022

A. Carys

CHAPTER TEN

May 2022

Today is the second day of the magic transfer, and it's been a rough process so far.

It's been a year and six months since I gave control of the Circus to Rosain and Rowyna. After watching them make quite the name for themselves when we were touring the other reality, and successfully organising another international tour, I believed that it was time to give them magic.

We began yesterday at sunrise, using the book of magic to help guide us. It's been a process, that's for sure. The three of us have to sit close to each other as I repeat the words of expulsion every ten minutes. There's a lot of magic to transfer and the book said we could be doing this for up to four days. Twelve hour transfer stints and twelve hour sleep stints to ensure that our bodies have time to rest and recover.

"Dad, it hurts," Rowyna says as the next lot of magic is transferred.

"I know it does, sweetheart, I know," I say as I reach over and squeeze her hand. "It'll all be over soon. I promise."

Rowyna looks pale. She's sweating and shivering all while Willow tends to her. Willow has been a rock, taking care of us and making sure we get everything that we need in order for this to be successful. Once she's finished with Rowyna she comes back over to me and sits in between my outstretched legs.

"How are you doing Ro?" I ask my son. He's been extremely quiet throughout this, the only sign that he's feeling anything is the few small whimpers that have been leaving his mouth.

"Yeah, I'm all good."

"Good. Just let me know if you're not."

Day two fades quickly into day three. The worst of the transfer is over now and Rowyna and Ro have more colour back in their faces. Their sleep was fitful throughout the first two days, so was Willow's, but thankfully the three of them are finally sleeping soundly. The twins are leant up against each other, while Willow is still between my legs, her back and head resting against my chest. The skin on my chest has been returning to its normal tone since most of the magic has left my body. I'm seeing tanned skin that I haven't seen in years, not since before I took on the magic of the circus.

A knock on the door draws my attention.

"Come in," I say quietly, trying not to wake everyone.

The door opens and Mr Myles steps through it. He gently closes the door before coming and crouching next to me.

"Mr Myles, nice to see you."

"You too kid, but I'm not here for friendly chatter."

I sigh. "Oh dear. Bad?"

"Very bad. Malory Alakaua and her brother Elias are extremely interested in the disappearances of not only the people here, the supposed Curse of Wesley Lane, and also the unrelated, very sudden upheaval and disappearance of Maeve Matson and her family."

"Well, I've never met Maeve Matson so I'm clear

on that one. How close is she to the others?"

"She's in the ballpark. She's not quite there yet but I wouldn't leave it too long before acting."

Damn it. "Okay. Send her an exclusive invite for next week's big showcase before we leave to go on tour again. I'll assess her then and I can have Ro and Rowyna deal with her."

"Of course. Anything else?"

"No, thank you, Mr Myles. You've been an asset for so many years that I'd like to gift you a holiday. Especially for whatever is decided for Malory and Elias. Wherever you want to go, just let me know."

"Thanks kid, that's very generous of you. But the pleasure is all mine, working with you have been the best years of my career."

I nod, smile, and shake his hand. "Till next week Mr Myles."

"Till next week."

A Circus of Wonder

ABOUT THE AUTHOR

A. Carys is a self-published author from Portsmouth, United Kingdom. Other than spending 90% of her day writing, she also loves to crochet, read, and take photos of her family's cats.

Printed in Great Britain
by Amazon